For Erica and Laura—
city mouse, country mouse!
—A.S.C.

HarperCollins®, ⬛®, and I Can Read Book® are trademarks of HarperCollins Publishers Inc.

Biscuit Visits the Big City Text copyright © 2006 by Alyssa Satin Capucilli Illustrations copyright © 2006 by Pat Schories All rights reserved. No part of this book may be used or reproduced in any manner whatsoever without written permission except in the case of brief quotations embodied in critical articles and reviews. Manufactured in China. For information address HarperCollins Children's Books, a division of HarperCollins Publishers, 195 Broadway, New York, NY 10007. www.harperchildrens.com
Library of Congress Cataloging-in-Publication Data
Capucilli, Alyssa Satin, 1957-
   Biscuit visits the big city / story by Alyssa Satin Capucilli ; pictures by Pat Schories.— 1st ed.
     p.   cm. — (My first I can read)
   Summary: On his first visit to the city, an excited puppy sees tall buildings, hears loud buses, and tries to say hello to everyone he meets.
   ISBN-10: 0-06-074164-3 — ISBN-10: 0-06-074165-1 (lib. bdg.)
   ISBN-13: 978-0-06-074164-8 — ISBN-13: 978-0-06-074165-5 (lib. bdg.)
   [1. Dogs—Fiction. 2. City and town life—Fiction.] I. Schories, Pat, ill. II. Title. III. Series: My first I can read book.
PZ7.C179Bist 2006   2005002662
[E]—dc22   CIP
                                                                                                                     AC

17 18 SCP 15 14 13   ❖   First Edition

Biscuit Visits the Big City

WITHDRAWN

story by ALYSSA SATIN CAPUCILLI
pictures by PAT SCHORIES

HarperCollins*Publishers*

Here we are, Biscuit.

Woof, woof!

We're in the big city.

We're going to visit
our friend Jack.

Woof, woof!

Coo, coo!

9

Stay with me, Biscuit.

It's very busy in the big city!

Woof, woof!

11

There are lots of tall buildings in the big city, Biscuit.
Woof, woof!

There are lots of people, too.
Woof, woof!

Funny puppy!
You want to say hello
to everyone.

Stay with me, Biscuit.

It's very busy here!

Woof, woof!

Beep! Beep!

Woof!

It's only a big bus, Biscuit.

Woof, woof!

You found the fountain,
Biscuit.

There's so much to see
in the big city,
isn't there, Biscuit?

Woof!

Coo, coo!

Woof, woof!
Coo, coo!

Woof, woof! Woof, woof!

Oh no, Biscuit! Come back!

Biscuit, where are you going?

Woof!

Silly puppy! Here you are.

This is a big, busy city, Biscuit.
But you found our friend Jack,
and some new friends, too!

Coo, coo!

Woof!